CROCUS TOWN

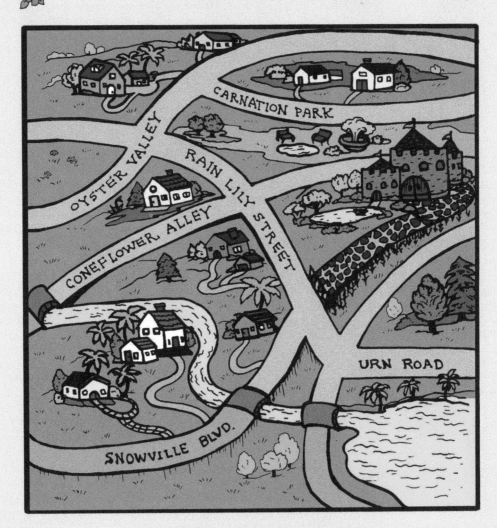

LIYA YOHANNES

AuthorHouse™
1663 Liberty Drive
Bloomington, IN 47403
www.authorhouse.com
Phone: 833-262-8899

Because of the dynamic nature of the Internet, any web addresses or links contained in this book may have changed
since publication and may no longer be valid. The views expressed in this work are solely those of the author and do
not necessarily reflect the views of the publisher, and the publisher hereby disclaims any responsibility for them.

Any people depicted in stock imagery provided by Getty Images are models,
and such images are being used for illustrative purposes only.
Certain stock imagery © Getty Images.

This book is printed on acid-free paper.

ISBN: 978-1-6655-3899-2 (sc)
ISBN: 978-1-6655-3898-5 (e)

Library of Congress Control Number: 2021919515

Print information available on the last page.

Published by AuthorHouse 09/21/2021

authorHOUSE®

CROCUS TOWN

CHAPTER 1

Royal High Boarding School

Today I woke up one hour before my alarm clock. Then I jumped up, went to the restroom, took a quick shower, went to the kitchen, and made breakfast for my mom, dad and me. I also whipped up coffee for my mom and made a milkshake for me, because I wanted to leave the house with a good vibe since I was leaving for four years. During breakfast, my mom and dad told me to be good at high school and follow my dreams of being a doctor and a writer. I was listening to half of the conversation, because I wanted to see my friends at the train station.

I was excited and nervous because it was our dream school. I waited for my mom to hurry up and take me to the train station. When my mom dropped me off, I started looking for Windy, my best friend. I saw her talking to Pearl—she's a part of our group and loves sewing.

"Hey guys," I said.

They said hi back, then someone squealed, "Rose!"

My name is Rosalynn, but my friends call me Rose. I looked around and saw Ruby and Chrystal. I asked, "Can you guys believe we're going to Royal High?"

"Nope," Chrys answered.

"Wow, I thought I was the first one here," said Rainbow.

"Rainbow, you're the last one here," said Ruby.

We all laughed. The train came five minutes after Rainbow showed up. We all went to the train, took our seats, and headed for school.

As soon as we got to school, we each went to our registration to gather information about who was going to be in the same dorm. Four students are allowed in each dorm, so we were all nervous to see if we were going to be the same dorm. Luckily the cards said Rosalynn, Opal, Windy, and Sasha will be in Room 105; Ruby, Chrystal, Pearl, and Grace will be in Room 106; and Rainbow, Dusk, Dawn, and Star will be in Room 107.

We were all happy that we were next to each other. We got our belongings and went to our rooms. Opal, Windy, Sasha, and I all looked around the room, and I said, "You all know that I don't like cooking."

Sasha said, "I've got the cooking part."

"Okay, let us go," said Opal as she organized our room.

We smiled and started our duties. After a couple of hours of working hard, our room looked amazing. Sasha prepared a yummy meal—vegetables for me and pasta for everyone. Our first day was fun.

Opal said, "I can't wait to meet all the professors that are going to teach us the next four years."

"Me too," said Sasha. We all agreed.

"I'm tired," said Windy, and we all said goodnight.

I said, "Don't forget to set up the alarm."

"Sweet dreams," said Windy.

CHAPTER 2
Earth

"Guys," said Opal, "time to get up. It is time for what we have all been waiting for, everybody."

Everybody scrambled up, and when I saw Opal was ready to go I asked her, "What time did you wake up?"

She smiled. "You know me, I am a morning person. Hurry up, breakfast is ready."

"Are you serious you made breakfast?"

"Of course. Cereal."

We all laughed at her good humor. I got up from my bed and dragged myself to bathroom. As soon as I took a cold shower, I felt awake, and my body relaxed. I am not a breakfast person, so I went into the kitchen and drank a glass of milk. Everyone was ready within thirty-five minutes.

I said, "Let us pray before we leave our room." We stood by the door in a circle and held hands together like we always do as I said our prayer.

When we left our dorm, I could see everyone was excited and nervous. When we got to the class, Opal said, "Good morning."

"Good morning," breathed our teacher. She was a tall woman with light pink hair and azure eyes. "My name is Cotton Candy, but you may call me Mrs. Candy."

She bowed. We all introduced ourselves and took our seats. After each of us introduced ourselves, the teacher started by telling us that because our next years are going to be awesome, our first day begins right now. We all laughed.

"Today we will learn about the earth, the forests, and the very ground itself," she began.

She taught us how important it is to keep our environments clean, about the Go Green initiative, and how Earth was mad at every living being because we all threw garbage of all kinds all over it—garbage that pollutes the soil. We all were so interested we didn't even know it was already lunchtime.

"Wow time flew by," said Sasha. She raised her hand. "Mrs. Candy, what are we learning about tomorrow?"

"Dear," Mrs. Candy replied. "It's a secret."

When we left, we all had a crucial question, "What will we learn about tomorrow?"

CHAPTER 3
Pollution

"Good morning, everyone," said our hyperactive teacher as she bounced up and down. She was wide awake and full of energy. In her right hand was an empty coffee cup.

Windy said, "I wonder why she's so much more hyper than yesterday."

Mrs. Candy squealed, "Today, we're learning about pollution. Pollution can be garbage, smoke, noise, and many other things. It is anything that makes the earth unhealthy and dirty. Air pollution is when the air gets dirty. It is caused by wildfires, industrial chemicals, smoke from cars, and other sources. Air pollution causes breathing problems and is also a cause of global warming."

"Oh, now I see why my brother has asthma," Sasha mumbled to herself.

"What's asthma?" questioned Windy.

Sasha replied, "It's a respiratory condition that makes it difficult to breathe."

"Exactly," I said.

Mrs. Candy continued, "Water pollution occurs when chemicals, waste and other gets into the water. There are natural causes also, such as volcanoes, animal waste, algae, silt from floods. It effects animals that survive in water, such as fish, crabs, and dolphins, as well as humans and other animals. It disrupts the food chains."

OMG! I exclaimed in my head.

"If sound becomes too loud or lasts too long, it becomes noise pollution. Noise that reaches a level of eighty-five decibels can cause hearing loss. Transportation like cars and jets, and household objects like the vacuum cleaner and mixer grinder make noise pollution. Natural events like heavy rains, earthquakes, and volcano eruptions can also lead humans to have anxiety, hypertension or hearing loss, or cause other disruptions like poor sleep."

"I now see why the earth is sad," said James, a curious boy who loves questions. We always call him Curious James.

"That's all for today, class. Goodbye!" Mrs. Candy announced.

"Goodbye, Mrs. Candy," we chorused back.

"We're free!" shouted Windy.

That afternoon, we planned to go to Lavender Beach.

CHAPTER 4
Lavender Beach

Lavender Beach is very popular in my kingdom. As we went there, Ruby got carsick.

"How are you carsick? You ride a motorcycle for goodness sake!" said Rainbow.

"Well, probably because motorcycles have fresh air!" said Ruby.

We all say, "That's because motorcycles have no windows!"

At the beach, I felt something calm, great and powerful, but I brushed it off. I looked at what my friends were doing. Pearl and Opal were surfing, Ruby was sunbathing, Chrystal and Sasha were eating ice pops, and Rainbow was making a sandcastle with Dawn. Everyone else was just at the dance party in Lavender Park, which was right next to the beach, and they were *very* noisy.

I saw a bit of light under a rock—well a small but heavy boulder. I picked the rock up, and I saw a staff underneath that had pink roses and forest green leaves. I felt like every forest in the world was calling to me. I picked it up and felt a surge of power. I gathered my friends to ask if they saw anything peculiar.

Sasha said, "I saw a heart shaped pendant, and I felt all the love in the world."

Ruby, Chrystal and Pearl said the same, but they all felt different things. Pearl said she saw a bracelet and felt like a raging tsunami, Ruby saw a bracelet and felt like an erupting volcano, and Chrys saw a bracelet and felt like an icy-cold cavern. When Windy saw a butterfly pendant, she felt like she could fly. Star felt like a star when she saw star earrings. Rainbow felt like she should help everyone when she saw a rainbow-colored hat. Only Grace said nothing. We all kept the things we found. After a long day, half of us got some ice cream and the other half got brownies. When we got back to our dorm, we saw Curious James.

James asked, "Who is cleaning the beach?"

Chrys answered, "Mermaids, duh!"

We all giggled and went to our dorms feeling triumphant. As I went down to my dorm Grace said to me, "I saw a ring, and it felt like I was the leader of every element.

"she yaned and said "

"AUUUUGGGHHH Good night."

Seriously What? The whole night I thought about what she said. *The whole night.* I got very little sleep.

The next day, I woke up early—earlier than Dawn, and man she is an early riser. "Hey guys!" I squealed. I drank a venti coffee already that morning.

"Get dressed," I said. I was already wearing the uniform.

After they got dressed, I thought my friends were thinking, *Who are you and what have you done to Rosalynn Earth?*

In class, Mrs. Candy was doing jump squats, and the tables were on the other side of the room. "Today, we will do P.E." She giggled.

At the end of class, I complained, "Today was *really* painful!"

"*No, it wasn't!*" shouted my friends.

"All *we* did was do jumping jacks and running!" shrieked Windy.

"Exactly!" I shouted. "It hurt my legs!"

"What's all this commotion about?" asked our teacher, Mrs. Candy. "Anyway, darlings, lunch." She laughed like a maniac just out of prison. "Did I scare you?" she asked. She saw us all trembling in fear as the bell rang.

Later,, I stopped by Mrs. Candy's office, the door was open I walked in I cleared my throat "Hello" I said to her she waved at me and said "What brings you here Rosie", I asked "Mrs. Candy, are there any magical staffs in Earth Kingdom history?"

"Yes, but there is only one magical staff in history, that is the ancestors of your kingdom., because I read about the staff. But no one has seen it since it was taken by a girl," Mrs. Candy replied.

"What is it called?" I asked.

"No one knows." She shook her head.

In my bed, I thought about what she said. "Could it be that I have found the one and only staff of the Earth Kingdom?" I whispered to myself. "Yeah, right," I added uncertainly.

CHAPTER 5
The Garden

I woke up and looked at my calendar. It was a Saturday, a weekend day. I woke up my friends by blowing a loud horn in their ears.

"Rooose, did you really have to wake us up?" complained Grace.

"Yes, we shall now choose where to go today."

"I've got the spinning wheel of our names. Who ever name the hand touches, we have to go where she wants, okay?" said Dusk.

"Ok," we all chorused.

"Hmm. Dawn, get it. It's next to my bed."

"It is?" she asked.

"Of course, why are you so surprised?"

"It's just when I look at your bed I see nothing."

"Oh, it's invisible," Dusk said.

"What?" I exclaimed.

"Now, go get it, Dawn. It's not invisible through the afternoon and nighttime."

"Oh."

She went and got it. It had all our names on it, and we use it when we have an argument. "Rainbow, spin it," Pearl ordered.

"Ok, boss," said Rainbow. She spun it, and it landed on my name.

"Oh, yes!" I screamed.

"Well, where do you want to go?" asked Windy.

"We shall go to A field of flowers," I announced. Everyone groaned. "Is there something you want to tell me?" I said

"No." everyone answered at the same time

"Ok let's eat" i said We all ate a wonderful batch of pancakes made by Sasha and changed into beautiful clothes. Chrys and Ruby wore yoga pants and took their yoga mats, so when they got to the field they could practice their flexibility.

We entered A Field of Flowers. "It's so peaceful," I said. *OMG*, I thought. *It's nothing like Eden Garden, but it is beyond beautiful. I have no words. It is magnificent.* Lavender flowers are colorful, but the first one that attracted my eye was the candy cane flowers—ornamental holiday blooms. I asked the tour guy, "Where is the rose?"

He said, "That is our last. We will keep the best for last. Autumn pink sorrel, Lelea flowers finally rose, and pride turned the field worthy with all the anemone, crocus and other types of flowers." My eyes are overwhelmed. The tour guy asked, "You must know the history about the rose?"

I said, "Yes, sir." All my friends' eyes were on me. "Is there anything you would like to tell us?"said Chrys

Mr. David, the tour guy, said, "One of you is the chosen one."

"What does that mean?" asked Curious James.

He explained, "If one of you finds a golden rose, you will be the master of Royal High. You will be the president of the student council."

Everyone ran around to find the golden rose. While I was looking, I saw a glowing, gold rose next to a glowing, pink amaryllis. Both stood out from all the rest. "You guys are beautiful," I said in awe. I got out my flower basket with all the different types of flowers in it. I grabbed the beautiful flowers, and I felt a powerful surge through my body.

"Whoa!"

I went to the candy cane sorrel field where my friends were. When I got there, I saw they were annoying the gardener of these fields with questions like "Do you garden *one* field?" and "Is it true you don't shave?"

"Guys, I got the golden rose!" I screamed.

"Okay!" they yelled back.

CHAPTER 6
Weekend Fever

The morning is bright, and I'm feeling energetic. Over breakfast, I planned my day. I realized I couldn't find Windy. For a minute, I thought they left me by myself. I saw her in the living room watching TV. "Why are you up so early?" I asked.

"Because it's Sunday."

"I forgot about your Sunday morning show. Oh, well, then I can go to the library and find some books on gardening, my plans for the next four years, and what I need to do."

The alarm clock woke everyone up except Pearl. "How is she still asleep after we honked a horn in her ear?" exclaimed Grace.

"I have an idea," said Dusk. "White Ice is signing books in Lightning Library!" she screamed.

Pearl woke up. White Ice is the name of her favorite novelist. "Where? I need to meet her," she said.

"Ahem," said Dawn.

"Oh, hi, everyone. Where's Lightning Library?"

"Right in Anemone Avenue, Street 142," said Sasha.

"Well, I am heading to Lightning Library. Anyone else want to come?" I asked.

"Me, bestie," said Windy.

"Literally all of us, especially Pearl," said Dusk. She smiled and rolled her eyes.

I hummed my favorite song, Roses, practically singing it to pass the time while we walked to the library.

"We're here," said Ruby.

When we entered the library, we saw the kind, sweet and helpful librarian cataloging the nonfiction section. "Hello, girls," she said when she saw us.

"Hello, Miss Thunder."

"Why are you here? For the computers, the flowers, the cookies, or the books?"

"The books, miss," said Dawn.

"Well, what kind of genre? Wait, I already know that. Rose wants the gardening books, Windy wants the tornado books, Ruby wants the action books, Pearl wants the novels, Chrystal wants the graphic novels, Star wants the space books, Dusk wants the nonfiction books, Dawn wants the—"

She saw us looking at her like, "Did you read my mind?"

"What?" she asked.

"It's just—how did you know?" asked Pearl

"That's what you ask for every time you come here."

"Oh," we all said.

"Now, please go up the stairs," she said.

We walked up to see a bunch of books. There were enough that I could give a hundred to all the kids at my school and still keep three hundred for myself.

"There are *so* many books," said Windy.

"Uh oh. Rosalynn's getting excited," said Pearl.

It was true. I love books, so it wasn't much of a surprise when this happened. I started bouncing around, nearly knocking my friends off their feet.

"*Stop.* Let's just borrow *one* book," said Sasha.

We all got one book from our favorite series. When we got downstairs, we showed her our IDs, borrowed a book, and went back to our dorms.

CHAPTER 7
The Exciting News

Monday morning, I woke up and changed into my uniform. That's when I heard the announcement. A sing-song voice said, "Hello, students. Come to the auditorium quickly. We have an announcement to make. Have a nice Monday."

"Oh," then I skidded to the Kitchen and made breakfast.

"Well, hello, Rose."

"Hi, Grace," I said.

"What's for breakfast," said Ruby as she ran in the kitchen.

"French toast."

"YEEEEEEEES!" said Grace. We both looked at her, confused. "Sorry," she said sheepishly. "It's just that I love French toast."

As soon as everyone woke and dressed, we ate and headed to the auditorium for the announcement. We saw a bunch of kids and teachers sitting down on the floor and on chairs, and we decided to sit on the floor. We saw the vice principal talking to all the teachers about some kind of trip. When everyone finally quieted down, and Dusk looked like she was thirsty for a book, the principal said in the same sing song voice I heard over the radio, "Hello, students. Here are the announcements. Firstly, for the eighth graders, Miss Darling is out sick, and her substitute is Miss Thunder, the Lightning Library librarian."

As soon as she said that, Miss Thunder walked on the stage and bowed. When Miss Thunder walked off the stage, the principal said, "Mrs. Candy's class will go on a trip to the Earth Kingdom. Rosalynn Earth's parents will be their tour guide."

That's when my parents walked on stage with my little sister and my brother, all smiling. They went off the stage, and the principal said some other things, but I wasn't listening. I was going to my home kingdom with my family. Once the announcements were over, my class started packing up for the trip.

CHAPTER 8
The Flight

"Guys, are you ready," said Ruby.

"Yep," shouted Mrs. Candy.

"Now *get on the plane*!" Pearl shouted.

"Jeez, boss," said Rainbow.

"Darling," said my mom, "are you okay?"

"No," I said.

I had a bag just in case I puked again, like my last trip across the world to a palace. Coincidently, I puked when I looked at the water a thousand miles down, disgusting my mama enough to make her puke in her bag she brought just in case my sister needed it.

"Ew," said my little sister. "What was that for?"

"Well, sis, some people have a fear of flying called aerophobia. They're scared of heights, so they get headaches or motion sickness, which can cause vomiting. That is why we have a bag—in case you or I are vomiting."

"Okay, got it. Thanks, big sis."

We heard our pilot say, "Hello, families and students. We will endure some rough winds, so put on your seat belts." Not wanting to die, we all buckled our seat belts.

Later, my little sister, Orchid, said, "I'm hungry, mommy."

"Orchid, mommy's sleeping," I said.

"Oh. Do you have an apple?"

"No, but you can ask Leaf."

"Big bro? I already asked him, but he said no."

"Oh," I said to my hungry sis. "Well, when we go home to our house, we can eat sweets and apples."

"Yay!" said Orchid, loud enough for the whole middle class to wake up.

"Shh, sweetie. Everyone's super sleepy from those winds, so please be quiet," I whispered.

"Oh," she said quietly.

The flight attendant came with apple pie and gave it to Orchid. That's when I was knocked out from exhaustion and sleepiness . Finally, after four hours, we landed in Rosemary Airport near Crocus Town.

CHAPTER 9
The Mystery

When we went to Crocus Town near the palace of the royals, we hardly saw any roses. "Where are the roses?" asked Mrs. Candy. "The roses were the whole reason we came here."

A shopkeeper said, "Have you not heard all the roses in all the towns are completely gone with no trace?"

Orchid said, "Thank you for this information." We all looked at the small child, baffled.

"And you're wrong. The thief did leave some tracks," I said "I remember when we saw millions of roses in the palace."

"WHAT?" yelled the shopkeeper.

"My dear, how do you shout so loud?" asked Dusk.

"My kids," the woman said. "And if you guys want, I can tell you where you are."

"We know Crocus Town," said Rainbow.

"No, you're in Coneflower Alley, and my name is Bellflower," the shopkeeper said before disappearing into thin air.

"Wait, how did she just disappear into thin air?" I asked my mama.

"Magic." My Mama shrugged.

We went to Rain Lily Street where the palace was. "The names of the king, queen and their two children are King Oyster, Queen Carnation, Princess Urn, and Princess Snowdrop. They have the power of the golden flowers and ancestors" my brother, Leaf, said, playing tour guide to my class. "Look here everyone this is a painting of the royal family"said Leaf. We looked at their smiling faces, their red and golden robes on them.

'Pay attention especially you sis" Leaf added,

Everyone looked at me then back to the painting .

''I felt some kind of connection to the painting ''i said ''it must be what Mrs. Candy was talking about the magic t'' I mumbled to myself

I looked over to a castle window and saw a guard talking to a person named Crocus. I discovered that my rose had true powers, and whenever I was near the Crocus guy I had an uneasy feeling. Almost all the names lead to Crocus. That's when I figured out he was the thief who stole all the magical roses in the kingdom. I confronted him the next day and asked why he did it, and what he said shocked me very much.

CHAPTER 10
The Surprise

He said, "Well, my people are extremely sick with a disease, because we have trashed the earth and it was mad at us. It started in one town, then started taking over cities. The only place it didn't take over is these twelve kingdoms, because you guys take care of it while having fun. I've warned my people, but they never seem to hear."

"Oh, I have something to ask. Is your name even Crocus?"

He laughed a pleasant laugh. "No, my real name is Asher, and yes, I am wearing a disguise." He pulled out his contacts and revealed his dark purple eyes were part of the disguise. His real eyes were hazel to match his long, chocolate-brown hair.

"So, what's the name of the disease?" I asked.

He said, "Immune killer." He frowned at the name.

"I've heard of it before. My Aunt Caroline died because of it," I said, also frowning.

When we were boarding the plane later, Orchid said goodbye to Asher, and we went inside the plane. We saw Mrs. Candy looking awfully ill, just like Aunt Caroline did before she died.

Meh, I thought. I went to my plane seat, and we headed back to school.

When we got back to the school, all the students at my school swarmed my whole class. They asked us how we were, and the whole class answered questions like "Did you meet the royal family?"

We heard the vice principal say in a strict voice, "Students, come to the auditorium now." We went as quickly as possible. The vice principal cleared his throat. He looked nervous and worried, and when he started talking, he shook. "Uh … uh …"

My friend asked, "OMG, what is he going to tell us?"

Finally, he told us the bad news. "Mrs. Candy is sick with a disease that is exceedingly rare, so she won't be in class. Also, the entire nation is on lockdown, so you will be going home. We already informed your parents. They are waiting for you outside. Go pack up your belongings, please follow the news and stay safe. Don't go outside until further notice. Any questions?"

Curious James raised his hand and asked, "How long are we going?"

"For about two months for now, but we don't know when we are coming back, and you will all stay home until we ask you to come."

My whole school started shouting, and I blacked out.

CHAPTER 11
The Letter

I was in bed, feeling sad because of what happened yesterday. I stood up, still moping, and went to the kitchen. My mom was outside watering Orchids flower and vegetable garden, and my dad entered the kitchen and started chopping raw carrots. Those were obvious for me, since I love carrots—especially raw ones. I knew he only did it to cheer me up, and I was happy.

My mom came in saying, "Orchid, give me my earrings right now, young lady!"

"Never!" said my sister.

"Mom, calm down. Remember your breathing techniques I taught you," I said. Those methods help Mom a lot, since she is a very angry lady. She started breathing in and out so she could calm down.

"Honey, please go to Rose's room," said my dad.

"Is it because my room is the perfect place to calm down?"

"Uhhh," said Leaf. My brother walked in, and I knew he had heard us.

My mom and dad shrugged while Orchid yelled "Yes!"

"Oh, be quiet!" I yelled back.

"HEY!"

Orchid ran out of my room and went to her room. I got up, walked up the stairs, and went toward Orchird's room. I saw her huddled with our dog, Sammy, and our cat, Shamrock, under her princess-like bed. She looked worried, while Sammy looked sad and happy mixed in one.

"Darling, are you okay?" I call Orchid that when she's sad to make her feel better.

"No!" she cried out. "I can't go to school and meet Eli," she calls her best friend, Elizabeth, Eli or Beth sometimes, "and I can't even see the art activities our teacher told us she made for us during the year. But we never got to do it." Then she burst into tears. Shamrock looked at her and started hissing, and Sammy started whimpering. Orchid added, "And I heard Mom and Dad say Aunt Violet's wedding was cancelled because of this illness."

"Darling, things might be tough right now, but it will eventually get better."

She sniffled. "Promise?" she asked in a tiny voice.

"Promise," I said in a sad but confident voice.

"Lynn, the mailman is here," Leaf said. That's what my brother calls me, so I knew it was him.

"So?"

"So, you have a letter from Lily."

Lily is the only person in our family who can tell the future, besides Uncle Simon. "Oh, then I'll get it," I said. I went downstairs and saw an envelope signed with a crystal-blue orchid with white tips. I knew it was Lily's, because that is one of her signatures after each letter, and I have a whole collection—mostly because she writes letters to me a lot. I opened it. It said:

> My dear Rose, there is something stirring that is happening in the nations. I need you and your friends to find out what the cure for this virus is. Use your rose and amaryllis and find out what it is. Please do it after two months. Oh, and do research about the virus, and if you need to go outside, wear a mask over your nose and keep a distance from strangers and people you know.
>
> Signed, Lily Violet

ACKNOWLEDGEMENT

I would like to thank my family for believing in me and trusting me so that I could make it happen dad (Yohannes Admassu) and my grandparents Tata and Baba (Getachew Kebede and Azeb Fantey) especially My Mom Zimam Kebede who believed in me that I could write this book and help the children in Africa and make my dreams come true and into shape Thankyou Mom love you

Liya

CPSIA information can be obtained
at www.ICGtesting.com
Printed in the USA
LVHW070831271021
701668LV00015B/817